llama llama learns to swim

Anna Dewdney

Based on the bestselling children's book series by Anna Dewdney

Penguin Young Readers Licenses
An Imprint of Penguin Random House

PENGUIN YOUNG READERS LICENSES
An Imprint of Penguin Random House LLC

ISBN 9781524787196   10 9 8 7 6 5 4 3 2 1

Llama Llama and his friends play in Luna Giraffe's backyard. Luna shows everyone her brand-new swimsuit.

"I have an idea!" she says. "Let's go to the beach!"

"A beach day sounds like fun!" says Nelly Gnu.

"We can go bodyboarding."

Gilroy, Euclid, and Luna are excited. But Llama Llama isn't so sure.

"You look nervous, Llama Llama," says Nelly. "Don't you want to go to the beach?"

"Well," says Llama. "I don't know if I like the beach. But it could be fun, right?"

"It's going to be a blast!" says Nelly.

That night, Llama Llama talks to Mama Llama. He tells her he is worried about going to the beach. "I'm afraid to go in the water," he says.

Mama Llama puts her arm around Llama's shoulder. "Is that because you don't know how to swim?" she asks. Llama nods.

"It's okay, honey," says Mama Llama. "Not knowing how to swim is nothing to be ashamed of. Would you like me to give you a swimming lesson?"

"Yes!" exclaims Llama Llama.

The next day, Llama and Mama go to Eleanor Elephant's house. She has a pool! Llama dips a foot in the water.

"Not bad, right?" asks Mama Llama.

"Actually, it's pretty nice!" says Llama.

Mama shows Llama some swimming strokes. Then Mama helps Llama float on the water. Finally, they both hold their breath and dip underwater together. Llama Llama likes learning to swim!

After their lesson, Llama and his Mama say "Goodbye!" and "Thank you!" to Eleanor. As they are leaving, Nelly and Luna walk by. "What were you two doing at Eleanor Elephant's house?" Luna asks.

Llama tells his friends the truth. "Mama was giving me a swimming lesson," he admits. "I was nervous about going to the beach because I don't know how to swim."

"We could all use a little practice before hitting the waves," says Nelly. "Mama Llama, will you give us a lesson, too?"

Mama Llama agrees.

The next day, Llama's friends join him for another swimming lesson.

There's even a surprise guest—Grandpa Llama!

Llama is confused. "Grandpa, what are you doing here?" he asks.

"Your mama told me you were afraid of getting in the water," says Grandpa. "Well, so am I! I never learned how to swim."

Llama Llama smiles. He can't believe it! But he's glad to have a swim buddy who is just as nervous as he is.

"We'll stick together, kiddo!" says Grandpa.

Llama and his friends practice different kinds of swimming strokes. Luna shows everyone how to dog-paddle. She kicks her legs and paddles her hands underwater.

Everyone else gives it a try. Dog-paddling is fun!

"Grandpa," says Llama, "we're *llama*-paddling!"

Grandpa laughs.

By the end of their lesson, Llama Llama and Grandpa Llama swim all the way across the pool. "You did it!" everyone cheers.

"You swim buddies are ready for the beach tomorrow!" Nelly says.

The next day at the beach, Llama Llama's friends are by his side.

"Don't worry," says Nelly. "You can do it."

"Just remember everything you learned at the pool," says Euclid.

"Okay," says Llama.

He takes a deep breath.

"Here goes!"

Llama wades into the water.
It is cold and wet. The sand
squishes under his feet.
It feels great!

But something is missing—
his swim buddy! "Where's
Grandpa?" Llama asks.

Llama sees his grandpa standing at the shore.
He is scared to get in the water!
"Oh no!" says Llama. "I have to help him!"

"There's a lot more water here than there was in the pool,"
Grandpa says nervously.

Llama Llama takes his grandpa's hand. "It's okay," says Llama.
"I'm your swim buddy, remember? I'll be right by your side."

Grandpa nods. "You're right," he says. "Let's do it!"

"One foot at a time," Llama says as they walk into the water.

"Hey, this feels pretty nice!" says Grandpa.

"Especially because we're doing it together," says Llama.

Llama Llama and Grandpa Llama float on the water.

They toss a beach ball back and forth with Llama's friends.

They're having so much fun! And then . . .

. . . they go bodyboarding!

"Everybody ready?" asks Nelly.

"Here comes the wave!"

Llama cheers. "Woo-hoo!"

"We're doing it!" says Grandpa.

21

Later, Llama Llama and Grandpa Llama visit Mama and Grandma Llama on the beach. "I'm really proud of you!" says Mama. "You faced your fears and got in the water. And now here you are, playing and swimming with everyone."

Llama Llama and Grandpa Llama both feel proud.

"Thanks, Mama!" says Llama.

"I guess you *can* teach an old llama new tricks!" says Grandpa.

"There's just one problem," says Grandpa Llama.

"We don't ever want to go home!"